MURPHY BEAR'S TENNIS LESSON

Written by MAURA MOYNIHAN

Illustrated by LEE BERZMAN

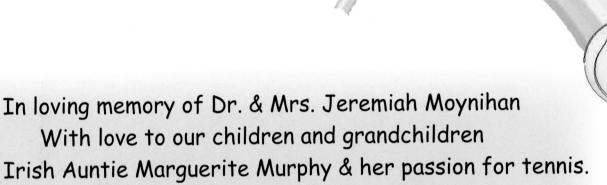

In loving memory of Dr. & Mrs. Jeremiah Moynihan
With love to our children and grandchildren
To my Irish Auntie Marguerite Murphy & her passion for tennis.
Thanks to Vic Braden & Chris Evert
for their inspiration.

The sky was blue as a robin's egg. Lemon lights lit the sun-room but Murphy stayed in his pajamas all day.

"Do you have the blahs?" asked Dad. "Are you down in the dumps?"

Murphy sighed, "My best friend moved far away."

"Get dressed," said Dad. "I have a surprise."

Outside Murphy's bedroom door was a shiny racquet.

"I signed you up for a tennis lesson today," said Dad.

"I don't know how to play tennis," grumbled Murphy.

"It's fun," urged Dad. "Soon you can join the tennis team and you will meet new friends."

Murphy's eyes grew wide. He bear hugged his dad and packed his bag.

Into gusty wind he pedaled hard, balancing like an acrobat. A pelican swooped in his path.

"*Look Out!*" called Murphy. "I don't want to be late for my first tennis lesson."

The pelican followed behind him.

Murphy arrived at the courts and met Miss Angel Hare, the tennis pro. Her teeth sparkled like sea shells and her eyes were black as tar.

"Call me Miss Angel," she said with a smile. "Let's start with a warm up. Just follow me."

Murphy copied Miss Angel as she stretched. "These are yoga poses," she explained. "Take deep breaths to feel calm and strong."

Murphy made his body into a triangle. He squatted like a chair and balanced into a tree pose.

"Beautiful," uttered Miss Angel. "Now get your racquet."

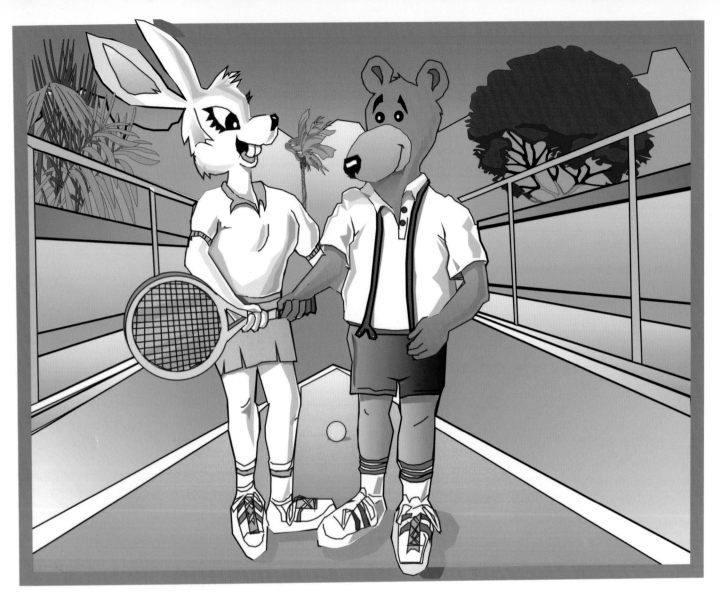

"First, I'll show you the **forehand grip.** It's like a handshake."

"Nice to meet you," Murphy joked, shaking the racquet.

Miss Angel giggled. "Don't squeeze too tight," she said. "Hold your grip as you would hold a baby bird."

Next, Murphy practiced watching the ball.

"The middle of the strings is called the **sweet spot**," she told him.

Murphy imagined his racquet dipped in warm chocolate with a cherry on top.

"*YUM*," he whispered. "I'm hungry." And the ball rolled off.

"Concentrate," urged Miss Angel. "Let's try to bounce the ball."
Murphy scrunched his eyebrows. "*CLUNK,*" the ball hit the racquet frame.
Then he heard, "*PING, PING,*" off the middle of the strings.
"You got it!" she said. "Now squeeze a ball to make your wrist strong."

At last, he learned the *forehand stroke*. Murphy started in the *ready position*,
"*feet apart, knees slightly bent and racquet head is level*"
Murphy hummed, "*racquet back* (turn shoulders) ... *step in* (with left foot)
... *then swing*." He swung his racquet, "*low to high!* "

Ready position   **Racquet back**   **Step in, then swing**

Then Miss Angel showed Murphy how to move his feet. "Pretend," she said, "you are standing on hot coals." "*OUCH!*" he joked. And he imagined her feet on fire. Murphy walked around the net to try the **forehand stroke**. "Are you ready?" she called.

Murphy didn't answer. "Can I do this?" he wondered.

The pesky pelican circled the court. Murphy looked up and sighed.

He took a deep breath and got in **_ready position_**.

"_OK!_ ", he finally answered.

Miss Angel called out, "Let the ball bounce once and then hit."

She tossed him a ball ...

"*SWISH!*" he missed and "*WOOSH!*" he missed again.

"It feels like there is a hole in my racquet," shouted Murphy.

"Keep your eyes on the ball," Miss Angel said in a calm voice. She tossed him a ball and...

"*SMACK!*" The ball hit the net tape. Murphy frowned.

"*Almost!*" she cheered. "Swing from your shoulder, bend both knees and follow through up high."

Murphy was thinking too hard about everything he had learned. He took his racquet back... stepped in... and...

"*OH NO!*" Murphy roared. His ball lobbed to the sky.

"You crazy bird!" Miss Angel gasped. "It's not a fish!" And she busted into laughter.

Murphy chased after it. "Drop my ball!" he demanded... But the pelican flew far away.

Out of breath, Murphy headed for the bench.

"I'm not very good at tennis," Murphy mumbled.

"It takes lots of practice," Miss Angel explained. "And your shot wasn't wrong. It's called a *lob* but it has to land inside the lines."

Murphy thought for a long time. He heard cheering from the next court. It was his neighbors, Erin Bear and Gavan Gator. They were having lots of fun playing tennis.

He finished his drink, took a big stretch and sighed, "I'll try again."

Miss Angel carried a punch bag onto the court.

"What is that for?" Murphy asked.

"This is your target," she said. "You can aim for it.
But first concentrate on hitting the ball over the net."

Murphy stood in *ready position*. She tossed him a ball and...

"PING!" he heard the sweet sound off the racquet strings.
The ball arced like a rainbow over the net.

"I did it!" Murphy said proudly.
"Great shot!" Miss Angel agreed.
And she fed him more balls.

Sometimes he missed, but he was
so excited he didn't give up. Then
all of a sudden...

"*POW!*" He hit the target right on the nose. Murphy pumped his fist and said, "*YES!*"

"*WOW!*" Miss Angel yelled. "Now it's time for a ball pick up," she announced. "Your lesson is over for today."

"Can I hit some more?" asked Murphy. "Tennis is fun!"

"Gavan Gator has a lesson next," Miss Angel answered. "But I can show you how to practice by yourself on a backboard. Let's fill the ball hopper as fast as we can."

Murphy ran and made his shirt like a pouch.

"You are a Kangaroo!" chuckled Miss Angel.

Murphy thanked Miss Angel.

"See you next week," she said. "Try to practice."

As Murphy jumped on his bike, he spotted something in the sky.

A shooting star tennis ball flashed through the blue.
"*THUMP!*" It landed in his bag. Murphy laughed so hard,
his handle bars wobbled.

"Someday I'll be a tennis champion," he thought.
And he coasted home, smelling salty sea air.

Over the next few weeks, Murphy practiced his tennis strokes on a backboard and took more lessons. His mom and dad gave him healthy snacks. But on the weekends he ate his favorite hot fudge sundaes. Then soon after...

Murphy joined the tennis team where he made lots of friends. Miss Angel Hare tacked a photo of Murphy Bear and his family inside the club house. The picture read. . .

Tennis, the sport for a lifetime!

Fantastic fun, forever fit

MURPHY'S TENNIS TIPS

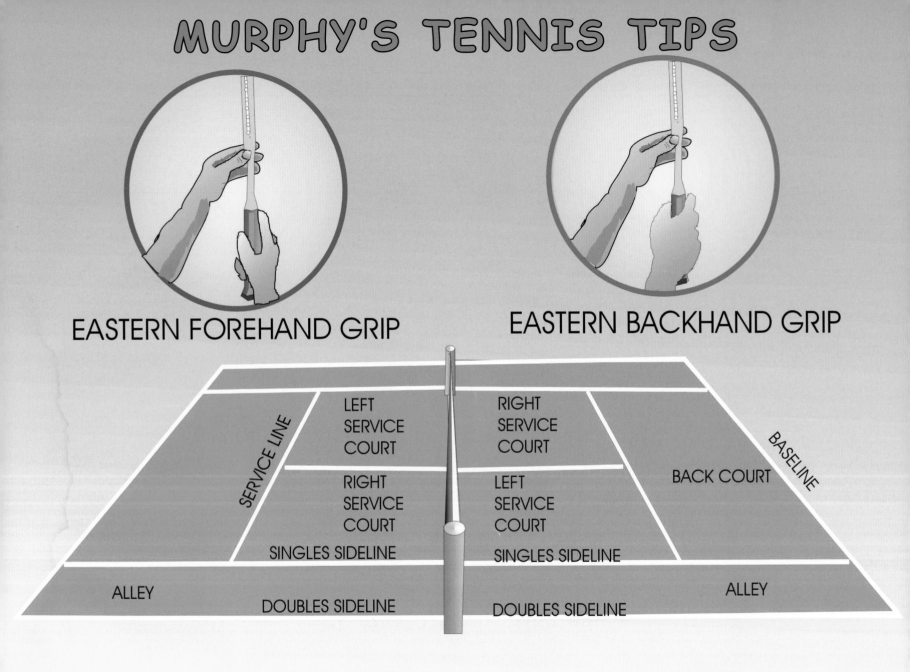

EASTERN FOREHAND GRIP

EASTERN BACKHAND GRIP

LEFT SERVICE COURT

RIGHT SERVICE COURT

SERVICE LINE

RIGHT SERVICE COURT

LEFT SERVICE COURT

BASELINE

BACK COURT

SINGLES SIDELINE

SINGLES SIDELINE

ALLEY

ALLEY

DOUBLES SIDELINE

DOUBLES SIDELINE

THE COURT

THE BACKHAND

LIKE THE FOREHAND IN THE STORY, BUT HIT FROM THE OPPOSITE SIDE.

Backhand grip - use a two handed or one handed backhand.
Start from the **ready position**.

1. Shoulders turn sideways bringing **racquet back**.

2. **Step in** toward the net with right foot.

3. **Then swing**.
   Contact the ball out in front, keeping racquet head level.
   Swing low to high.

THE SERVE

Follow the eight boxes. The grip is called "Continental" or middle grip. Stay loose.

Stand behind the baseline and turn sideways to the net.

Toss the ball from your left fingertips and toss over front foot to one o'clock.

Imagine that you are throwing the racquet over the net.

Hit the ball at the height of the toss.

Step in and finish across your body.

THE VOLLEY
A BALL HIT IN THE AIR AT THE NET

1. Serve grip. Ready position
(Hands up and out in front).

2. Forehand volley
Cross Step with left foot and *block* ball (no swing).

3. Backhand volley
Cross Step with right foot and *block* ball (no swing).

At the start of the game each player has zero or "love".
The first point is 15.
The second point is 30.
The third point is 40.
The fourth point is "game".

Singles is a tennis match between two players.
Doubles is a match between four players, two on each team.

A set goes to the first player who wins six games. He must win by two games or play a tie breaker at six games all.
A tennis match is won by the player to win two out of three sets.

If the score is tied at 40-40, it is called "deuce".
Now one player must score two points in a row to win. The player to win the first point has the "advantage". If he wins the next point, it's "game". Otherwise it's back to "deuce".

THE SCORE